ISLINGTON

Please return this item on or before the last date stamped below or you may be liable to overdue charges. To renew an item call the number below, or access the online catalogue at www.islington.gov.uk/libraries. You will need your library membership number and PIN number.

12|14

Islington Libraries

020 7527 6900   www.

D1379974

First Published in 2013 by:
Pneuma Springs Publishing

Aliens and Angels Three Stories For Christmas
Copyright © 2013   Sue Hampton
ISBN13: 9781782283157

Sue Hampton has asserted her right under the Copyright, Designs and Patents Act, 1988, to be identified as Author of this Work

British Library Cataloguing in Publication Data. A catalogue record for this book is available from the British Library.

Pneuma Springs Publishing
A Subsidiary of Pneuma Springs Ltd.
7 Groveherst Road, Dartford Kent, DA1 5JD.
E: admin@pneumasprings.co.uk
W: www.pneumasprings.co.uk

Credits

ALIENS AND ANGELS is illustrated by Sue Hampton, who also designed the cover.

NOT WITHOUT A CARROT features drawings by pupils at Victoria First School, Berkhamsted.

BOOTEE FOR ETTA has been illustrated by pupils at Greenway First School, Berkhamsted.

Sue would like to thank everyone who helped and hopes they all had fun.

Aliens and Angels

Robbie sat on a big plastic throne.

"It swivels, look," said his mum, giving it a little push.

But Robbie didn't feel like spinning. He didn't want to be there. Around his shoulders was a towel that caught the drips from his long, fair, curly hair. In the huge mirror that filled one wall, Robbie saw his mouth wobble.

"I don't want a haircut now," he said.

"You'll be so smart you won't

know yourself," said the barber, loudly and cheerfully.

Robbie stared up at him. *Not know himself?!* Wouldn't that be a bad thing, and scary? He was used to himself the way he was.

Robbie's mum said they were there now, and if his hair got any longer the teacher would plait it, or put it into pigtails with ribbons.

The barber laughed but Robbie thought that would be fun.

"You can't head the ball into goal like that!" said the barber, rubbing his head a bit drier. He was rough, especially around Robbie's ears.

"I don't like football much anyway," said Robbie.

"Of course you do," said his mum, and the barber joined in as he picked up the scissors.

Robbie frowned up at them both, one on his right and one on his left. How did they know? They weren't there at playtimes.

Robbie preferred dancing.

Suddenly the scissors were slicing away hair. Thick curls formed crescents on the towel, like soft moons, yellow and warm. Some settled on the floor, where the wind tugged at them when someone opened the door to the high street.

"Have you got your Christmas presents yet?" the barber asked Robbie's mum. "People keep telling me there are only twenty-four shopping days to go."

Robbie's frown lifted. Christmas! Yay! Santa, a tree and a stocking, decorations and parties and best of all, the nativity play.

But he would never get the role he wanted. Robbie made a squished face that his mum called a pout. His eyes looked back at him from the mirror, wider and brighter than usual.

He'd never be an angel now.

Fifteen minutes later, Robbie was gripping the arms of the chair so he wouldn't cry. From the mirror, a boy was staring – as if he'd never seen him before in his life. The barber was right. Robbie didn't know that boy! He had a smaller, flatter, harder head. He had bigger ears and sad eyes.

It was a boy who could be a shepherd with a tea towel on his head, or a king with a cardboard crown, but not an angel.

Robbie felt sorry for that boy.

"You'll get used to it, Rob," said his mum as they left.

"I don't want to," murmured Robbie into the wind that beat around his cold neck.

As he trudged home, Robbie didn't care about the street lights shining in the twilight ready for Christmas. His hair didn't move anymore and his feet didn't want to dance.

At school the next day the other boys laughed the moment they saw him in the playground. Fingers pointed. Mouths turned into big red tunnels. Eyes bulged.

"About time!" said Freddie. "My mum said you looked like a girl."

"Still does," said Jay, and the others laughed.

But as they hung up their coats, Sanamir whispered, "You still have lovely hair."

Hannah said, "It'll grow back ever so quickly. Mine did."

Hannah's hair was long and straight. When they were a bit younger, she used to stroke his head and he stroked hers because they both felt soft, but different.

Robbie hoped she was right, but now there were only eighteen days till the school play. He'd counted on the calendar.

At lunchtime that day their teacher, Miss Hussain, told them they would start rehearsals that afternoon. Sanamir and Hannah put their hands together and shook them with excitement. Miss Hussain read out the parts.

Sanamir would be Mary. She looked just right, especially when she smiled like that. Freddie was Joseph but he didn't look too pleased.

"I don't want to marry *her*," he muttered, loud enough for Sanamir to hear but not Miss Hussain.

"You're mean," Robbie mouthed at him.

The kings, shepherds and innkeepers were called out. Robbie waited, but still his name wasn't called. What about the angels?

He stopped prodding the rubber with a pencil.

Could it be? Was it possible?

"Hannah, I'd like you to be the chief angel," said Miss Hussain. "Also angels: Lily, Jocasta, Soraya, Maddie, Lucy, Sarah and ..."

Robbie looked up, saying his name silently, his eyes on Miss Hussain's list.

"Ah yes, Javeen."

Javeen looked relieved. Maybe she'd been worried about being the back or front of the donkey. Robbie tore a hole right through the rubber.

Michael, the best reader in the class, was a TV presenter who needed a camera crew. Miss Hussain named them all but Robbie still hadn't been given a part.

"This year, there are aliens too," the teacher added, "so everyone else is an extra-terrestrial, but Robbie, you're the chief globalob."

Everyone laughed but some of the laughs were too loud and sharp in Robbie's cold ears. They weren't kind.

Robbie's cheeks felt hot.

"How many legs has a globalob got?" asked Charlie.

"How many heads?" asked Freddie.

"*Robies an alien orlredi*," wrote Jay on his whiteboard.

There were aliens that crawled, and aliens that zigzagged, but globalobs hopped. That was because, to answer Charlie's question, globalobs had just one leg. They were going to have their human legs tied together inside their costume but Miss Hussain said they could practise hopping at home.

"That sounds fun," said Robbie's mum after school that day.

"I could have been an angel," said Robbie, "if I hadn't had a haircut."

"They always choose girls for angels, Rob," said his mum. "Sorry."

Robbie knew that was true but it didn't make it fair.

"You're my angel anyway," said his mum.

She kissed the top of his head because she couldn't stroke her fingers through his curls anymore.

Later, when his dad was home, Robbie heard him laughing in the kitchen. Robbie thought he might be the joke.

"Why does he want to be an angel anyway, for goodness' sake?" he heard his dad ask.

"Shhh," said his mum, and he didn't hear the answer.

But as he lay in bed, Robbie thought of a few.

Because angels looked gentle and kind, so their dances were always dreamy and graceful, to starry music.

Because angels looked beautiful too, so they wore shiny white robes with glittery swirls and wide sleeves.

Because angels could fly, so they had smooth golden wings that shone. They didn't just walk – or hop on one leg. They had to dance as if they were light and bright. They had to dance as if the stage was the sky and they were gliding and swirling and soaring through it.

Nobody ever laughed at an angel.

It was more or less against the law.

But angels wouldn't care if they did.

Robbie would never be an angel so he'd better be a funny, crazy, clumsy globalob instead.

Over the next seventeen days there were lots of good things going on at home and school. In the classroom everyone had to make a snowman for the wall. Robbie drew big white wings for his, with silver stars. He cut round curly hair to give the head ice-creamy curves.

"A snow angel!" said Hannah, and Sanamir murmured, "Aw, sweet!"

"Aw, sweet!" jeered Freddie.

"What a lovely idea," said Miss Hussain. "Beautiful and different."

Next morning when Robbie looked for his snow angel on the white wall, he found it up in the black sky, among the moon and the stars. Hannah, Sanamir, Sarah and Maddie all gave him a smile.

So did Jay, but it was an ugly one, too ugly for the globbiest globalob.

There were decorations to make for the corridor. Miss Hussain said she had two ideas and showed them how to make both. One was a fat, red robin with tissue feathers and a 3D beak. The other was a golden angel.

Most of the girls chose angels, and stuck on long hair of yellow wool or felt. So did Robbie.

"It looks just like you," said Freddie.

"Angels are boys anyway," said Hannah, "in the story. There's one called Gabriel, not Gabrielle."

"Is there one called Robbie?" asked Jay. "Is he the prettiest angel of all?"

"Yes," said Hannah, "and the kindest."

That made the boys pull faces, and soon Hannah and Robbie were both blushing.

In Monday's rehearsal for the nativity play, the crawling aliens banged bottoms. But the biggest laugh came when Robbie

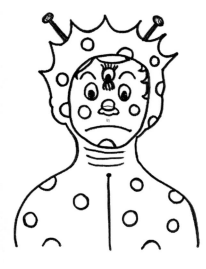

forgot to hop on stage with the other globalobs. He was too busy watching the angel dance, and making angel arms.

On Tuesday the zigzagging aliens got so tangled they toppled and tumbled. But the biggest laugh came when the teaching assistant told the chief globalob he looked 'about as scary as a butterfly'.

On Wednesday the little town of Bethlehem came unstuck from the night sky and made the angels jump. But the biggest laugh came later, when Jay gave Robbie a sneaky push from behind.

The chief globalob kicked the first King's gold towards the front row – and into Miss Hussain's lap.

"Gold!" called Hannah.

"That's the only goal Robbie's ever scored!" said Freddie.

"Miss Hussain saved it," Jay pointed out.

On Thursday the moon fell down from among the stars and rolled around the stage like a big coin until Joseph stamped on it. But the biggest laugh came when Robbie tried a globalob growl.

"You're meant to sound wild as a tiger, Robbie," said Miss Hussain, "not as cute as a kitten."

In Friday's rehearsal, things were going quite well until one of the shepherds tripped over his crook and fell into the chief globalob. Robbie ended up on top of the manger and some straw poked up his nose.

By this time, Robbie knew the angel dance step by tiptoed step and spin by airy spin. In his bedroom he made up extra bits that were so light his parents didn't hear a thing downstairs.

But however much he practised grunting, growling, hopping and punching the air, he was a rubbish globalob. Robbie wished for a tummy bug to save him but he felt perfectly well, just sad.

Then the night before the dress rehearsal, Robbie had an odd feeling that brushed away the sadness inside him and made him grin. No sooner had he closed his eyes than he heard a sound like a squelchy drum. Spotty globalobs were thumping around him, smacking the air and chuckling. They were kicking out their legs and piling up on top of each other.

One globalob seemed to be in charge. It was the noisiest and craziest, and hopped the highest. In fact, it hopped right over the red frogs and the green rabbits. It smacked the white leaves that swirled

through the air with its globalob fists and a "Gerrrroarrrr-ahoo!"

As it hopped along a river bank it tilted backwards with a laugh and a splash into the purple water. Out of its mouth rose a spray of round, shiny, purple bubbles. Robbie saw tiny fish darting around inside each one.

Robbie leaned forward, caught a bubble and laughed. The fish popped out and flew away into the branches of some wobbly blue trees, where they grunted happily.

The globablob was still in the purple river, wading, slipping, sliding and splashing. Suddenly its globalob gurgle sounded worried. It thrashed about helplessly.

Robbie reached out a hand and helped it out.

"Thanks, Robbie!" said the globablob, and under its green spots he saw a smile he knew.

Hannah laughed and hopped away, right into the sliding doors of a silver spaceship with orange spots. Robbie smiled as he waved it goodbye.

Rolling over under his duvet, Robbie opened his eyes. His back wasn't exactly itchy like it was when he had chicken pox spots, but it tingled. As he lay in bed, he felt lighter than a summer cloud, and softer too. On his pillow his head seemed to be floating.

"Robbie," said a voice.

Was it the TV downstairs? The voice sounded close enough to be inside his head. It sounded as quiet as the flowers in his garden.

Just above his head he felt something like a hand, not quite touching. It was very warm.

Robbie turned. There, behind him, was a tall, golden figure. It wasn't solid like his bed. It melted into the darkness like candle flame. Tall, shimmering wings pointed upwards to his bedroom ceiling. Their feathery white surface stirred like grass in a breeze.

The angel's hair wasn't long or short, but it glowed around its head.

"Are you a boy or a girl?" Robbie asked, because he couldn't tell.

"I'm just an angel," it said.

"Why are you here?" asked Robbie. His mum hadn't had a baby in the night, had she?

"I've come to tell you something, Robbie," said the angel. "You can fly."

Robbie smiled. "Can I?"

"If that's what you want to do, no one can stop you."

The angel laid a hand on his right shoulder, and as it rested there, he felt the tingle on his back grow warm and stretchy. The angel laid a hand on his left shoulder, and the skin behind started to twitch and stretch just the same.

He was growing wings, and they were wiggling and pushing out into the air, like moles scrabbling out of earth. They weren't tall and perfect like the angel's, but they were white and bright.

"Give me your hand," said the angel.

Then Robbie spread his wings, like a swan. They were light enough and strong enough to lift him right off the carpet.

Robbie was flying.

"I told you," said the angel.

Robbie's bedroom wasn't big enough for soaring and gliding. As the walls melted away he found himself out in the silvery darkness lit by the moon. He flew above his house, his street and his town, smiling down on all of them. He felt peaceful and light and free.

Suddenly a waterfall of brightness rushed him back into his bedroom. But where was the angel? Robbie was alone. A few flecks of golden light fizzed round his bed like the stars from sparklers. Then they danced out through his window into the winter night.

Robbie watched them disappear as he felt his head rest on his pillow. His wings had gone but his bedroom had never felt so still or so safe.

At breakfast next day, Robbie was bouncy with excitement.

"Dress rehearsal today, isn't it?" asked his mum.

"Oh yes," said Robbie.

He'd be wearing a stretchy, spotty costume instead of a beautiful angel gown but he didn't really mind. He'd have to hop in it, when he'd rather dance, but he didn't really care. He could fly and no one could stop him.

On the carpet, waiting for the register, he saw Hannah wave. She came and sat next to him.

"I'm always an angel," she said. "I wish I was a globalob. In my dream I was a mad one."

Robbie stared.

"You saved me," said Hannah. "You had wings."

Robbie stared again. Hannah winked, and put up her hand.

As the last parents and grandparents edged into the back of the school hall for the show, the lights went down. The chief globalob squeezed the chief angel's hand. The angel squeezed back.

The play began on other planets. The zigzagging aliens zigzagged very sharply. The crawling aliens wiggled their bottoms neatly, with no bumps at all.

When the leader of the spotty, one-legged globalobs hopped onto the stage, everyone gasped. She hopped higher than a kangaroo and her growl was fiercer than a lion's. When she punched the air, toddlers squealed. Laughter filled the hall and Hannah was so happy she very nearly joined in.

Once the aliens had all set off for Bethlehem in their spaceship, the lights grew softer. Gentle, starry music filled the silence. Onto the quiet stage glided an angel in white. Gold stars glittered on his gown and little wings gleamed over his shoulders. Spinning and swirling on tiptoe, the angel leapt, lifting graceful arms to stroke the air.

Alone, the angel danced more beautifully than he had ever danced in his bedroom. He very nearly flew. As he lifted his hands in a curve above his bowed head, he had never felt so happy.

Robbie held out one angel hand to the others, and they fluttered on to make a circle around him. When the music stopped, the audience clapped and cheered, and some people – including Robbie's dad – stamped their feet and roared.

"What a beautiful angel!" cried a granny in the front row. "Hoorah!" yelled Miss Hussain.

At the end of the play, everyone stepped forward for a bow. Last of all, Miss H u s s a i n beckoned the angels back. Robbie bent his knees and lowered his head. This time the cheers were even louder than before. A toddler covered his ears. Robbie thought the walls might wobble to the floor any minute. A hall full of globalobs couldn't make any more noise.

But inside Robbie's head he heard a voice lighter than snow.

"Robbie, you can fly."

He spread his wings and smiled. The chief globalob winked as she whooped.

Robbie lifted his arms and did a final angel spin.

"Nothing can stop you, Robbie," he heard, as he bowed again.

Hannah was jumping now, clapping with her feet as well as her hands.

"Don't forget, Robbie," he heard, even though the words were soft as butterflies settling inside his head. "Nothing ever will."

Robbie smiled, because now he knew. Nothing ever would.

NOT WITHOUT A CARROT!

Once there was a country where the sun burned all day long, and the houses were as white as salt. On the tops of those flat white houses, people dried things in the fierce sun. They dried the clothes they'd washed in the river and the dates and figs they'd picked from the trees.

In that country people had to work very hard just to live. They had to travel miles to collect water from a well. They had to walk all day to take their pots or rugs or olives to market.

There were no lorries or trains to take heavy loads. But life was much easier with a donkey.

Donkeys were tough. They kept going even when the sun was hot and the ground was rocky. And Trouble was the toughest donkey of all.

Donkeys were safe and steady. They didn't rear and toss their riders off. They didn't gallop about or charge around. And Trouble was the steadiest, safest donkey of all.

Donkeys were easy to feed because they ate the rough, dry, spiky things other animals wouldn't eat. They also fed on oats and barley. And as a special treat, they liked carrots. Sweet, crunchy, juicy carrots! Trouble adored them! Carrots had their own special smell on the air.

They had their own special colour, bright enough for a king's cloak. And when Trouble chomped them between big yellow teeth, they had their own special sound inside her head.

Trouble the donkey loved carrots. She was crazy about them. She daydreamed of carrots. She dreamed of carrots. She'd do anything for a carrot. As long as she had a carrot to look forward to, she was no trouble at all.

But there was a reason why Trouble's master called her Trouble – not Dusty or Starlight or Pebble. If Jacob wanted a job done, and he'd run out of carrots, he had no chance. He could sweet-talk Trouble but she'd shake her head. He could tickle her chin but she wouldn't budge. He could ask and plead and give her orders but it made no difference. She stood as stiff as a frozen lake. She kept her hooves as still as boulders.

It didn't matter what he wanted her to do. It didn't make any difference if he tugged at the reins. Even if he lost his temper and beat her with a stick, it had no effect at all. The answer was always the same.

"NOT WITHOUT A CARROT!" she said.

One day Jacob needed Trouble to take him to town to buy some hens. He offered her oats but oats wouldn't do.

"NOT WITHOUT A CARROT!" she said.

He offered her barley but barley wouldn't do.

"NOT WITHOUT A CARROT!" she said.

Jacob sighed. He'd run out of carrots. He borrowed his neighbour's horse but it pranced friskily and was hard to control. It kicked its back legs in the air every time it saw a snake. Jacob missed Trouble. He bought three hens and some cloth for his wife and came home with his nerves a-jangle.

"Did you remember to buy carrots?" asked his wife.

"Oh no!" said Jacob. "I forgot."

So the next day, when he had another job for Trouble, he begged in vain.

"Please, Trouble!"

"NOT WITHOUT A CARROT!"

Jacob sighed. Other donkeys did what they were told. Other donkeys made do with thistles if they had to. He decided that Trouble would have to go.

"She's a nice, comfy ride," said Miriam, his wife. "I could almost fall asleep on her back."

"She'll have to go!" said Jacob. "She's too much … trouble."

"Don't sell the donkey," his wife told him. "Just remember to buy plenty of carrots!"

While Jacob walked from farm to farm, hoping to find a fine crop of carrots, his wife Miriam tried to coax Trouble.

"Take me to the well, dearest Trouble," she purred in one pointed ear, "so we can both have a long cool drink."

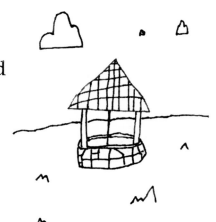

Trouble thought about it. She was hot. She was thirsty. She liked long, cool drinks.

But there was one thing she liked more.

"NOT WITHOUT A CARROT!" she said.

Miriam sighed and huffed and grumbled to herself. And when Jacob came back late that night with as many carrots as he could carry in a big basket on his head, she told him she'd changed her mind.

"Trouble will have to go," she said.

At that moment all the carrots fell from her husband's head and landed on their feet.

"OW!" cried Jacob, hopping. "I'll take her to Nazareth. I'll get a good price for her there."

"If you're going to Nazareth," said Miriam excitedly, "buy me a wooden chest from Joseph the carpenter. Please."

"Not without a carrot," joked Jacob, and she stuck one in his mouth.

When Jacob told Trouble they were going to Nazareth, she had something to say about it.

"NOT WITHOUT A CARROT!" she said.

"I've got carrots," said Jacob, and fed her one.

So Trouble agreed. It was a long journey but she gave him a nice smooth ride and they got there in record time.

The market was a busy, colourful, noisy place. Hens clucked and cackled. Sheep gathered in woolly huddles. Piles of firewood were stacked high. There were clay pots and jars, woven rugs and sandals for sale. And there was music in the air. Trouble heard the beat of drums, louder than hooves. Boys blew reedy tunes out of pipes.

Jacob remembered what Miriam had asked him to buy her. He asked around for Joseph the carpenter. Soon he found the workshop where he made his tables and chairs, chests and boxes. He waited with Trouble in the doorway. Trouble's nostrils quivered at the scent of fresh wood in the air.

Joseph the carpenter soon showed Jacob a finely carved chest for his wife's blankets and clothes. He asked a fair price and the deal was almost done when Joseph winked at Trouble the donkey.

"I need a donkey," he told Jacob. "Is she a good worker?"

"Oh yes," said Jacob. "No trouble at all - as long as you keep carrots in the house."

Joseph laughed, and when he patted Trouble's back, she knew he would never beat her.

"What do you think, Mary?" he asked the girl who was watching.

Mary crossed over to say hullo to Trouble. She smiled at her, and stroked her nose.

"I like her," she told Joseph, rubbing her gently under her chin.

And Trouble looked in her eyes and liked her too. Soon Trouble had a new home, a new master and a new mistress. That night, before she went to sleep, Mary brought her something. She held it out for Trouble to snuffle carefully from her hand.

"Sweet dreams, Trouble," she told her.

Mary smoothed the curve of her tummy, and even though she didn't say *yum*, Trouble wondered whether she liked carrots too.

Life with Mary and Joseph turned out to be just as good as Trouble thought it would be. No more beatings. There were plenty of strokes and tickles, and carrots too. Trouble slept at one end of the small, flat

house, like part of the family. And she was no trouble at all.

Sometimes Mary talked to her while she patted or brushed her coat. Trouble liked the soft breath in her ears even when she didn't understand the words. She knew Mary was glad about something because of the light in her eyes. And she knew she was excited, because of the lifts and jumps in her voice.

"I'm going to have a baby, Trouble," she said. "And I trust you completely. You're going to carry me – and the baby inside me – all the way to Bethlehem."

Trouble didn't know anything about Bethlehem. She didn't know much about babies either. But she knew the journey must take days and nights because every time Joseph came out of the house he had something else for her to carry. And Trouble knew that load included carrots.

She could smell them even before Mary whispered, "Plenty of carrots, Trouble," in one ear.

"It's a good job I'm tough," she said, proudly,  when she saw the mats and rugs rolled up and tied onto her back.

"It's a good job I'm strong," she said, when she was loaded up with figs, dates, olives and flat bread.

"It's a good job I'm careful where I put my hooves," she said, when Joseph helped Mary onto her back.

Trouble couldn't see the baby, but she knew it must be there somewhere, inside Mary's cloak.

Trouble took every rocky road and sloping track very carefully. The bundles bounced against her sides but she was proud to carry Mary, mile after mile, hour after hour. By the time it grew dark, she was glad to rest. Joseph led her to the river for a long drink. Then they unrolled their mats and sat and ate their food. Trouble didn't mind the beans and barley, but she made a little snort of delight when Joseph presented her with a particularly delicious carrot.

"You deserve it, Trouble," he told her, over the crunching of busy teeth.

So it went on, day after day. Sometimes Trouble wondered whether the journey would ever end. But she never stumbled, and she never complained, because she knew Mary must be tired too.

And then, one bright afternoon, Joseph pointed ahead with his stick. A small white town gleamed between the hills.

"Look!" he cried. "Bethlehem!"

Bethlehem was busier than an anthill. The streets were packed – not just with people and donkeys, but camels too.

"Look after Mary," Joseph told her, "while I find a place to stay."

Mary was so tired she was almost asleep on Trouble's back. Trouble kept very still and quiet, but she'd never been in such a noisy place.

Every time Joseph returned he was shaking his head.

"No one has any room," he said. "Bethlehem's full up."

"I'm not," thought Trouble. "I'm ravenous, and I could do with a whole mountain of carrots."

Joseph kept on trying, but soon it was dark. Now Trouble was worried too. She knew Mary needed a place to rest.

At last they found one. It was really for animals, not people. It wasn't an inn, and it had no beds – just straw on the earth floor. But it had a roof, and from the doorway Trouble could feel the warmth inside. Joseph lifted Mary down from her back.

Trouble poked her nose into the stable. But what she saw, heard, and smelt in the darkness made her jerk her head back again, as if a bee had stung her.

It wasn't the bleats of the silly sheep that bothered her. It was the thudding

tread of giant feet. There was a deep rumble from a throat she couldn't see. Half-hidden in the darkness were shuffling, lumbering oxen. To Trouble they were like great hairy caves on legs. The stable was steamy with their nasty breath.

Trouble's hooves were firmly on the ground. Her neck was stiff and her head did not move. She wasn't going one step further.

"Come on in, Trouble," said Joseph.

"NOT WITHOUT A CARROT!" thought Trouble, but her mouth stayed firmly closed.

Mary turned back to stroke her.

"Thank you, Trouble," she said. "We couldn't have got here without you."

Trouble's body loosened. She lowered her ears for Mary to tickle. Joseph held up a lantern and in its light Trouble saw the eyes of the other animals turning towards her. The sounds seemed softer now. She felt safer. The world felt still.

Trouble let Joseph lead her in. He looked for a place for Mary to sleep, but as she lay carefully down she remembered something.

"I'm sorry, Trouble," she said. "There are no carrots left. Can you wait until morning? Then Joseph will buy you the best carrots in town."

Trouble snorted. Could she wait? Would she sleep at all, with carrots on her mind?

She didn't say, "Not without a carrot!" because she was too exhausted. But if there were no carrots in the morning, she wasn't going to lift another hoof.

Trouble did fall asleep, in the end. But she woke, rather suddenly. It wasn't hunger that woke her, even though she had been dreaming of carrots. It was a feeling. Trouble didn't know what it was, but it stirred her somewhere deeper down than her stomach. It was like sleepiness and wide-awake play, both at the same time. It was stillness and something like danger. It was a wild kind of peace.

By the light of Joseph's lantern Trouble could see Mary's smile. The moon chinked in through the roof and walls, but the light that scattered the darkness was

buttery, almost hot. She heard the lift of wings as if all the birds on a silvered lake were taking flight.

"Look, Trouble," she said. "It's a boy."

Trouble stumbled up and took a few steps closer to see what was wrapped in her arms. The bundle was no bigger than a basket to carry eggs. But as Joseph leaned in with the lantern Trouble saw a small, dark face. The baby had come! His mouth  opened as if he might sing. But the sound he made was more like water bubbling around rock.

"We're going to call him Jesus," said Mary, and Joseph put his arm around her.

Then he knelt, the way people did sometimes, when they didn't know what else to do.

Trouble wanted Mary and Joseph to know she was happy too, happier than she'd ever been. She was happy just to watch and be.

Suddenly Mary remembered something.

"Oh, Joseph," she said. "I promised Trouble a carrot. A whole pile of them! She's been so faithful ..."

"It's midnight, Mary," said Joseph. "I can't buy carrots now. I think Trouble can wait till morning, can't you, girl?"

Trouble's head lifted high. Her ears grew tall and stiff.

"Carrots?" she laughed. "CARROTS?"

Trouble threw her head back and gave a snort.

The baby made a sound of his own, as if he shared the joke. But Trouble's laugh was louder and spikier, and came from deep in her throat.

"WHO CARES ABOUT A CARROT?" she thought. "Not me!"

She nudged her head towards the baby.

"Not any more!"

Joseph ruffled Trouble's neck. Soon everyone slept. Outside, the moon drifted slowly away over the hills and the sun rose fiery in the morning sky. Maybe

Trouble was the last to wake again. She looked for the baby.

Where had he gone? Was there danger after all? Her head turned anxiously, her ears fidgety.

Mary's eyes helped her find him. Jesus was in the manger, with hay around his head. Trouble saw his small brown eyes were open too.

Joseph brought Trouble a bucket of cool water and she took a slow drink.

"It's a new morning, Trouble," said Joseph. "And we promised you breakfast. Come on. We're going to find you the tastiest carrots in Bethlehem."

He picked up the bridle from the straw and nodded his head towards the doorway.

"Are you coming, then?"

Trouble remembered being hungry. She remembered how juicy carrots were and how much she liked the sound they made inside her head.
She lifted her hooves, but one step later she placed them very firmly down again.

She looked back towards the manger.

Her neck grew stiff and her head was high.

Trouble wasn't going anywhere. "NOT WITHOUT THE BABY!" she said.

Sue Hampton

BOOTEE FOR ETTA

Even before Etta opened her eyes, the feeling was wrong inside her. Then she looked around. Etta Gray was used to unicorns flying around starry cotton curtains. But the roller blind at the window was the colour of cold tea. This wasn't Etta's room because it wasn't her house. And the new morning didn't feel like Christmas at all.

Between the lumpy bed and the door were stacks of boxes, a baby buggy and a bouncy baby chair. Against the wall was a flat-pack with a drawing of a cot on its side. Etta would have liked a baby to cuddle but there wasn't one. Kalina, who lived in this house, only had a son called Pavel. He was ten and since Etta arrived on Christmas Eve he hadn't smiled at her once.

There was no stocking on the end of the bed because Santa wouldn't know she was here. Etta tried not to cry.

"Be brave for Mummy," her daddy had said, from America.

Etta wondered whether her mummy was awake too. It scared her to imagine the hospital bed with her mother in it, with her eyes closed.

When Etta's toes touched the carpet it felt flat as a playground, and nearly as hard. At home Etta had a rug that was as fluffy as Jumper, the lamb she loved. But she'd left Jumper behind. She hoped he was comfy on her pillow but she wasn't sure he'd sleep without her to cuddle him. Etta

always took Jumper away with her but this time everything was sudden. It had been too hard to think properly, with her mummy being carried away in the ambulance and Kalina asking about a toothbrush and pyjamas.

Etta cleaned her teeth, and then put on her dark blue velvet party dress that had been hanging on her own door ready to wear for Christmas Day. Her mummy would want her to look special. She put on her best lacy ankle socks, and gave her straight hair plenty of brushstrokes before she caught it up in a ponytail with a bluebell bobble.

"Etta? You all right? Come down for breakfast."

Kalina wasn't pretty like Etta's mummy and her voice was deep and scratchy, but she was kind. Whenever she came to clean, Etta's mummy gave her English lessons and called her a good pupil. Sometimes Etta's daddy asked on the phone, "How's Kalina the cleaner?" as if it was a joke, but Etta could tell her mummy didn't like it. She called Kalina a friend.

Even though it was Christmas morning Kalina wore a sweatshirt and jeans, just like she did when she vacuumed and mopped. Her husband, Milan, was peeling potatoes. He didn't talk much because he had something called depression, but he winked at her and waved the peeler.

"Happy Christmas, Etta," said Kalina. "Don't you look lovely!"

Etta didn't answer.

"I know it's not the same for you without Mummy but hoping maybe we visit later."

Etta said, "Mm."

"Maybe Christmas movie on TV," said Kalina. "You can take your breakfast in the lounge if you wish."

The wall that faced the little garden was thudding. Etta saw Pavel kicking a ball at it, as hard as he could. He looked fierce. Etta turned on the TV and watched some carols being sung in a church. Her mummy always played the piano on Christmas Day, and liked *Silent Night* best. Etta closed her eyes and imagined her making the music. But Pavel's football kept on thumping through it.

There was a string of red tinsel over the TV. Beside it stood a tree but it wasn't real, just white plastic with purple baubles hanging from its spiky arms. Etta could pat this tree on the head even though she was only five, and the shortest in the class.

Etta's mummy always said Christmas was magical but now Etta knew it wasn't really. If it was, her mum wouldn't be in hospital. Her dad wouldn't be stuck in New York, waiting for a flight home. They'd be together opening their stockings with Jumper.

The banging stopped and Pavel came indoors. Etta heard him talking in the kitchen.

"I'd forgotten she was here," he said.

He spoke like an English boy, a mean one.

"Shhh!" said Kalina. "Poor thing must be worried, and used to things fancier. We don't put on much of a show."

She came and stood in the doorway with her apron on.

"Shall we pull the crackers now, Etta?" she asked. "You think Milan look royal in paper crown?"

Etta shrugged. She was afraid of crackers but she didn't want Pavel to know that. Milan came in too, wiping his hands on a tea towel. Kalina let Etta choose first. She picked out the silver one and Kalina grabbed the other end. Etta shut her eyes tightly and leaned away. The bang was really just a quick snap but it made her jump.

She was left holding half the torn silver wrap. The others put on their hats.

"King Pavel!" said Pavel, standing tall in his yellow crown. "You're my servants."

"Think again," murmured Milan.

Pavel blew the tiny whistle that fell from his cracker, up close to Etta's face. The sharp noise made Etta hunch her shoulders round her head. Milan said something in Bulgarian and Pavel looked moody. Kalina pinned on a plastic brooch of a bendy holly leaf. It had two berries but one broke off and rolled under the sofa.

"How much did you pay for that load of rubbish?" asked Pavel.

"Go back to bed," said Kalina, "if you choose to be wet cloth."

Pavel huffed and went upstairs. Kalina asked Etta what kind of gift she had in her cracker. At first Etta couldn't find anything but then she felt a little lump inside. She pulled it out and sat it on the palm of one hand.

"Oh," said Kalina, "that's so pretty."

It was a box, a tiny one, with soft green sides that felt like grass. The box smelt like grass too – summer grass, just cut. It was so light that if Etta closed her eyes she could hardly feel it sitting there.

Milan stood watching Etta and the green box.

"Do you think there's anything inside?" he asked.

Etta didn't know he had such a soft voice and she'd never seen him smile before.

"It's too small," said Etta.

"Big enough for a pea," said Milan. "Maybe three. Or seven baked beans."

"The sauce would leak out," said Etta.

Milan rubbed his shiny head on the top where there was no hair. "Good point," he said. "Will you open it and see?"

Etta held it up to her ear but there was no buzz so it wasn't a bumble bee. For a moment she thought she heard a different kind of sound. Milan was waiting but Etta shook her head.

"It might be a disappointment," she said.

"You may be right indeed," said Milan. "Very wise words."

He sighed and went back to his potatoes. But Etta couldn't put the box down. She was sure it felt warm, as if whatever was inside had a heart. It was something very small and very light. The box tipped on her hand as if something moved inside it.

Etta stared at the box but she didn't lift the lid. Then Pavel bounded downstairs and caught her wondering.

"What's in there?"

Etta kept the box by her chest. "Don't," she said. "You'll hurt it."

Pavel grinned. "Is it a little girlie fairy?"

Etta hadn't thought of that but it might be.

"Let's see, then," he said. "Do little girlie fairies like music?" He put the whistle in his mouth ready to blow. "That's my cracker really. It would be, if you weren't here."

Etta didn't want the box now anyway. She thrust it at Pavel, walked past him and headed for the kitchen. But before she got there she heard a gasp from the lounge. It was shaky and high enough to be a scream but Pavel held it back. Turning, she saw how white his face was. He jumped onto the sofa, and froze there. He looked as if he was stuck to the back of it and would climb up the wall if he could.

The tiny box lay on its side on the carpet but the lid was still shut. The whistle lay beside it.

"Mouse!" he breathed. "It's got a creepy little tail and creepy whiskers!"

Etta gave him a puzzled look. She couldn't see any mouse. She just picked up the box and took it up to the bedroom that wasn't hers. She lay on the bed and sat it on her tummy. Suddenly it almost bounced. Etta couldn't hear any claws but she wouldn't be afraid if she did.

Etta opened the box. For a moment she thought it was filled by a fluffy ball of cotton wool. Then she heard a bleat as a tiny white head lifted up and leaned over the edge of the box. Black eyes the size of full-stops gleamed at her. Four tiny legs sprang up. They were no thicker than wool but they were strong enough to scramble. The tiny white animal jumped out of the box into the palm of Etta's hand. It was a lamb, just like Jumper. But this lamb was no bigger than the bobble round Etta's ponytail.

Etta was afraid to stroke his woolly head in case her finger felt like a tree crashing down on it. The lamb might be woolly like Jumper but she didn't suppose he was wearing enough wool to knit a sock – except for a baby.

"Hello, Bootee," she said, and smiled, because the lamb was a beauty too. "Happy Christmas!"

Bootee looked happy. Etta could see he was a playful lamb who wanted to frisk and frolic so she carried him downstairs in her deep velvet pocket.

"May I go in the garden, please?" she asked.

"Wish I could come," said Milan. "I still got another fifty potatoes to peel – and they just for Pavel!"

Kalina said she must wrap up warm so she put on her coat and little boots. To keep Bootee a secret, she sat him on her head under her hood. Outside, she checked no one was at the window. Then she lifted him down. He sprang out of her hands in his hurry, and began to gobble grass.

This garden was no bigger than a mattress for a grown-up bed. But it was wild and weedy enough to feed a whole flock of Bootees. Etta almost lost him because the bright green blades of grass towered around him. The ground was muddy and soon Bootee was looking rather brown and slimy. Etta took him to the outside tap for a shower but the water gushed out too hard and knocked the lamb out of her hand. She had to catch him quickly before he landed on a stinging nettle or a prickle.

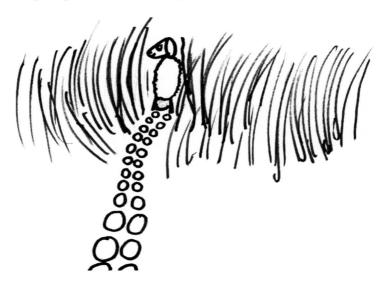

Bootee was going to need lots of care and attention – and first of all he needed a blow dry. Maybe Kalina had a hairdryer she could borrow.

A window opened.

"Etta! Is your daddy!" called Milan.

Etta almost jumped like a lamb herself. Bootee was nibbling leaves in the vegetable patch and didn't want to be scooped up when she tried. Leaving him to feast, she ran indoors. But her daddy wasn't there. He was only on the phone.

"Honey," he said, "are you all right? Is it Christmas there?"

"Not really," said Etta.

"I'm at the airport now, Etta, and it's stopped snowing so the planes are flying again. I'll be home before you know it."

But Christmas would be over by then. Why didn't he come before? Why did he have to work in America anyway? She'd heard her mum ask her auntie that.

"Mummy will be all right, sweetheart," he told her.

"I want to see her," said Etta.

"You'll be able to visit soon," he said, "I'm sure."

Etta knew he didn't know. He was in New York. He asked to have a word with 'Kalina the Cleaner' so Etta told him not to call her that and ran back outside.

Where was Bootee? She shouldn't have left him! Etta searched low down, in the grass and among the bushes, but it was a brown and green world with no trace of white wool. A sound made her look up. Balancing along the top of the fence was a black cat with a droopy tummy. It turned its head to look at her with cold green eyes before it dropped down next-door.

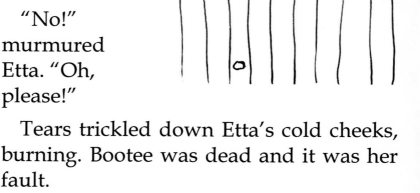

"No!" murmured Etta. "Oh, please!"

Tears trickled down Etta's cold cheeks, burning. Bootee was dead and it was her fault.

She went inside, and as she kicked her boots off at the back door she pretended she hadn't heard Kalina say her name. Etta went to lie down on the lumpy bed – the bed where she'd left the little box. But the box had gone. Etta turned her face towards the wall, wishing she could sleep and sleep until she woke up at home with her mummy and daddy. Jumper would be on her pillow, leaping about with excitement. All of this would be just a dream.

"Etta," called Kalina outside the spare room door, "would you like a chocolate?"

"No, thank you," she said.

"They're my chocolates anyway," she heard Pavel say.

"Come down and play games," said Kalina. "The chicken's in the oven."

"It's meant to be turkey," said Pavel. "We never do anything the proper English way."

Etta went down to the lounge. Pavel was complaining that they didn't have a proper garden so he couldn't play football. He called that 'the beautiful game'.

"What games you play, Etta?" asked Kalina.

"Scrabble," she said, because her daddy taught her a year ago and called her a Christmas star.

"Charades!" cried Pavel, and explained in Bulgarian. "Me first!"

Etta sat on the sofa watching him without really seeing. Kalina kept calling out suggestions but Pavel always shook his head as if they were silly. He seemed to be acting some kind of baddie and it made him scarier than ever. Milan pulled down his mouth and covered his eyes.

"What can we do, Etta," he whispered, "to make the day nicer?"

Etta thought it would be nice if Pavel went to sleep.

"My little green box has gone," she said instead.

Pavel stopped his charade, muttered that it was Deadly Attack 2, and flopped back on the other sofa looking sulky. Milan disappeared, but a moment later he was back, with the box in his hand.

"I don't know how it ended up in the compost bin," he said. "I give it a wipe but is bit of a mess."

Pavel gasped and ran out of the room as if the baddies in Deadly Attack 2 were hunting him.

"Mouse alert!" he yelled from the top of the stairs. "Get a trap! Feed it to the cat next-door!"

"There's no mouse," Etta told Milan. "There never was."

"Pavel thinking tough guy but in fact very terrified of mice," said Milan. "Sometimes people imagine thing we fear most."

Etta pictured her mum in the hospital bed with tubes coming in and out of her skin and machines bleeping. That was scarier than a million mice. Her mum would have loved Bootee. She might have opened her eyes just to see him.

Now the soft green box smelt of raw onion. The little grass walls were splashed with coffee grinds and tomato seeds. Etta wiped the bits away with a tissue from her pocket but the box only made her sad now.

Soon Christmas dinner was ready and Kalina was singing along to pop songs  about snow and reindeer. Pavel covered his ears. He scowled when Kalina served Etta first.

"You're giving her the crispiest potatoes!"

Etta wasn't hungry anyway. She poked a sprout into the gravy. Suppose her mummy was asleep and missed Christmas dinner?

"Please may I have a lie down?" she asked.

Kalina said she would keep her plate warm in the oven in case she fancied it later. She patted Pavel's hand with one end of the oven gloves to stop him stealing Etta's potatoes with his fork. Etta went up to the spare room.

As soon as she stepped through the doorway she smelt something, but it wasn't onion. The room had the scent of a whole forest of bluebells. The grass box was on the bed, and it looked brighter and greener than ever. Not a trace of mess. Only a magic box could clean itself. She breathed in and smiled as she picked it up. The box jumped in her hand.

As she lifted the lid, Bootee put up his front legs and began to clamber out. Etta helped him. He was as clean and white as brand new snow. Bootee was so excited that when he skipped up and down her thighs and tummy it was a bit like dancing. There was a metal tray on its side against the bedroom wall, so she put it on the bed and stood Bootee on it. His hooves made a clipping rhythm as he gamboled around.

"Bootee, you're a tap dancer!" Etta told him. She was hungry after all. "Come on."

Kalina and Milan seemed pleased to see her but Pavel didn't. Etta sat at the table with a Christmas napkin on her lap, and as she ate, she carefully dropped tidbits for the lamb in her pocket. One sprout leaf landed on his head but he managed to knock it off and catch it in his mouth. The pudding crumbs were nearly as big as he was, so his little white tummy must be getting very full. Her pocket was starting to bulge. After lunch, they all

watched TV. Milan fell asleep. A music show came on and Pavel did dance moves to the pop songs. Kalina ate chocolates.

Milan snored very suddenly. Then Bootee snored too, inside Etta's pocket. She felt the vibration as if her swollen pocket would rip. But the sound was as quiet as a snowflake landing on a piano key.

There was a much louder sound from the hallway. The phone! Kalina went to answer it.

Etta tried to listen but it was hard with Pavel pretending the carpet was a trampoline. Shouting, "Yeah!" and "Hey!" he looked as if he was aiming to punch the ceiling with his fists. A vase shook on the shelf. Etta thought Bootee could dance much better.

Milan woke jerkily.

"Give me ballet," he said, and tried to twirl on pointy toes until he fell back onto the sofa.

"Etta," said Kalina, smiling in the doorway, "we going see Mummy."

In Etta's pocket, Bootee's legs kicked with happiness. When Etta reached the landing he leapt out and ran ahead of her, his tail wagging friskily behind him.

Grabbing him before Pavel saw, Etta cuddled him to her chest the way she cuddled Jumper every night. He felt as soft as ever.

Pavel stayed with his dad while Kalina took Etta to the hospital, but it wasn't much fun in the lounge. Milan kept nodding off.

"Dopey," muttered Pavel. His dad was no fun anymore. He pulled at his arm. "Can we go to the park? I want to use my new football."

"Later," said Milan, in Bulgarian. "Stomach too full just now."

Pavel gave up and went upstairs. Glancing into the spare room, he saw the green box on the bed. Pavel frowned. Why couldn't his dad have left it in the compost bin where he'd thrown it? What if the mouse had come back? He put the whistle in his mouth ready to blast.

He tiptoed over to the box but as he drew closer he could see it wasn't really green. It was yellow as butter, like the baby buggy. It was made of squidgy plastic, the sort that wouldn't hurt if a baby threw it. Pavel squeezed it. Why did it feel so warm?

Lifting the lid very nervously, Pavel was ready to scream. The whistle dropped right out of his mouth onto the carpet. Something lay sleeping inside the box but it wasn't a mouse. It had no fur and no tail, but it was nearly as tiny. It had a tuft of black hair like his but its eyes were shut so he couldn't see whether they were brown too. Pavel breathed in hard. He was looking at a baby.

Pavel's mouth opened wide to scream but no sound came out. His baby sister was never born. She never grew any bigger. And he wasn't sad like his mum and dad because he didn't need a sister to spoil things.

This baby was alive. He could see it breathing inside a tiny baby-grow. One arm stretched out towards Pavel. Carefully he let his finger tip meet the baby's hand.

Inside him the scream had broken up. As he breathed, the pieces blew away and inside there was no tightness left. Pavel wrapped his hands around the burger-sized baby, trying not to squeeze. Two brown eyes opened and a mouth as small as an eyelash curled up in a smile. Two legs wriggled.

The baby was so small it would need protecting. Pavel found a hankie Etta had left behind. It seemed clean so he folded it for a mattress under the baby and laid it in the box. Placing the baby on top of it, he wondered how to keep his sister warm.

"Hang on, Sis!" he told her.

Pavel went to look for wool. Knitting couldn't be that hard. He'd seen his mum do it, when the baby was growing inside her, but the jumpers and dresses she'd knitted would bury the tiny baby in the yellow box. He rummaged in Kalina's bags but the wool was too boring and the needles were way too big. Picking up the smallest pair, he tucked them under his arms so as not to scare the baby. She'd think they were javelins!

Pavel crept back to the box in case the baby was asleep. Even before he looked inside he knew she had gone. But she'd left something behind.

Wool spilt out of the box like spaghetti. It was fluffy to touch, soft as the clouds might be, but glowing with colour. Not just red but orange and yellow. Not just green but blue, melting into a darker purple and a pale flowery mauve. They were rainbow colours, all of them, blending brightly into each other as if sun shone through every inch. As Pavel felt the wool, it flowed through his fingers like warm water – and ran away, swirling up through the air. It twirled out of the door and onto the landing.

Pavel laughed out loud, and chased it, waving the knitting needles like the conductor of an orchestra.

"Dad!" he called.

The wool ringed the air round his head, wove the air around his ankles and rushed down the banister like a rainbow waterfall.

At the bottom of the stairs his dad was laughing too. The wool wrapped itself into big, bright balls and landed in the palms of Milan's hands. Like reflections on water, the colours danced on his forehead.

"I'm going to make Mum a scarf," said Pavel, grabbing his sunglasses.

"Good idea," said Milan, and the wool seemed to agree. The first thread unravelled and cast onto Pavel's needles.

They laughed again.

"Also good dream," said Milan, as the first rainbow row clicked softly into place.

Etta's father sat on the plane, thinking that no flight had ever felt so long. Food arrived on a tray but he didn't want it. In a couple of hours he'd be landing at Heathrow and looking for a taxi to the hospital. It was the worst Christmas Day of his life but it wasn't over yet, not quite.

The roll was dry and he was too tired to chew. But what was this, wrapped in gold paper behind the cutlery and the yogurt? A present from the airline?

Jonathan Gray unwrapped the present and stared. His sleepy eyes peeled open wide. The box he uncovered was not much bigger than the mini pot of leftover jam. But tiny as it was, it was stunning!

Its small square faces were packed with jewels and mirrors. As he turned the box in his hand, they caught the lights from above his seat. Every bit of each surface was covered with something sparkling. The stiff patterns around it were stitched in metallic thread that glittered. Jonathan had done his Christmas shopping in the biggest stores in New York, but he'd seen nothing like this. What was it worth? Had they given one to every passenger?

He looked around, but there were no other boxes. The plane would be dancing with jewel light. It would be full of gasps! So where had his gift come from? Stroking its textures, Jonathan shivered. The shine was cold as ice. What could be in it? Something enormously expensive!

He had waited long enough. He felt like a Christmas child again as he lifted the heavy lid. For a moment the light that bounced off its walls was so thick and golden it blinded him. Then, like fog, it cleared.

The box was empty. Jonathan shook it, just to be sure. Nothing. Nothing at all.

A flight attendant came to take his tray and he passed it up to her, wondering whether the box was worth keeping. But only paper napkins, plastic cutlery and empty pots slid around on the tray. No box.

"Did Santa bring you something nice?"

The lady had seen the gold wrapping, tipped into the bin bag with everything else.

"I wish!" said Jonathan.

What did he wish? So many things. That it hadn't snowed so heavily in New York. That he was home with Jenny and Etta, instead of in this plane. That Jenny hadn't been taken ill on Christmas Eve. That he didn't live so much of his life on the other side of the Atlantic, making money. He'd been trying to be a big success with a name that counted. But he'd lost sight of the only thing that counted, in the end.

Jonathan remembered the cold, heavy, beautiful box. Like his life it was fine, and empty.

Pavel's knitting was going well. Milan helped him out with a row or two now and then, but it was quick-grow wool, almost magic really. It could be long enough by the time Kalina came home.

His mum would be surprised. It was ages since he'd made her anything and this would be the best present ever.

His dad gave him a thumbs-up. "Weather much better. Would you like park, with new football? I got my energy back. Beat you three-nil."

"Yeah, cool," said Pavel, laughing. "Just a few more rows."

In the hospital carols played softly. *Silent Night*! Etta hoped her mummy wasn't crying. Holding Kalina's hand, she smelt orange and spices. The floors were long and shiny and the walls were white but there were stars on the windows.

"This way," she told Kalina, because the arrow pointed ahead to CHRISTMAS. They pushed the door of a big ward full of beds.

"Mummy!" she cried, and ran.

Ahead of her went Bootee, tail swinging. Etta thought that must be what frolicking meant. The lamb reached the bed before her and sprang up onto the blanket. Her mum didn't seem to see Bootee, though. She reached out her arms and they only had room for Etta.

There was still a tube and a machine but her mum was sitting up, leaning against her pillow. She looked the way she did most mornings, before she'd brushed her hair or put on her lipstick. Not scary at all. She felt just the same to hug.

Kalina had stayed in the doorway but Etta's mum called her over.

"I'll never be able to thank you enough, Kalina," she said. "But I'll keep thinking until I find a way."

The three of them chatted for a while, and Bootee played on the hills that the blanket made over the patient's legs. Etta had never seen him quite so frisky. She noticed that he kept turning his petal-sized white head towards the door, and bleated whenever a visitor arrived for someone else.

Suddenly the white tail started to beat a fast new rhythm. Bootee ran towards the door, and leapt up at the smart trouser legs of a man with a suitcase. Etta's daddy didn't seem to mind. Etta charged towards him. Putting down the case, he lifted her as if she was no heavier than a fairy for the top of the tree.

Then he set her down on the end of the bed. As Bootee leapt into her lap for a stroke, Etta's daddy kissed her mum.

"I was telling Kalina," said Jenny, "how grateful we are for the way she called the ambulance and took good care of Etta."

Nodding, Jonathan took off his coat. He was shaking Kalina's hand when something fell out of his pocket. As it landed on the bed, the gold paper unwrapped itself. The little, heavy box was even more dazzling than it had been on his breakfast tray. Could it be made of gold?

He picked it up. If it was, Kalina deserved it.

"A small thank you, Kalina," he said.

Etta saw the way her mum smiled at him. Kalina's eyes were as bright as the stones and mirrors on the box.

"Thank you!" she said. "It looks... magical!" She lifted the lid.

"I'm afraid it's empty," Jonathan warned her.

Bootee bleated excitedly. Etta saw his black eyes turn to stare. She saw Kalina's lips part and her hands lift. She was smiling all over.

Kalina felt her face bathed by sunshine. Out of the tiny box floated an arc of coloured light, rising up and curving down again. Every colour was there, melting into the next: red, orange, yellow, green, blue, indigo and violet. Around it a watery haze broke softly away. Kalina watched as the rainbow led out of the hospital into the darkness.

"No," said Kalina, winking at Etta. "No empty at all. Full!"

"Yes," said Jonathan Gray, "A fool is exactly what I've been."

"No, Daddy, full!" cried Etta.

She laughed in his ear as she wrapped herself around his neck.

About Sue Hampton

Once nominated for Teacher of the Year, Sue became a full-time author after her first novel, SPIRIT AND FIRE, was praised by her hero Michael Morpurgo as "enthralling". He has also acclaimed JUST FOR ONE DAY as "terrific" and THE WATERHOUSE GIRL, in which Sue draws on her own experience of alopecia, as "beautifully written".

TRACES, which like POMP AND CIRCUMSTANCES is a crossover novel, was runner-up in the People's Book Prize, 2011 – 2012. Sue lives in Herts with her new husband, author and poet Leslie Tate.

Connect with Sue Hampton

For details of her other work, for adults, teenagers and children, see www.suehamptonauthor.co.uk

Other Book(s) by Sue Hampton

Pomp and Circumstances, ISBN 9781782281818

On Royal Wedding Day James isn't in the mood for romance after a disastrous date. His little sister's off to Hyde Park, and somewhere in the crowd he won't be joining is a girl from a different kind of postcode who could change his world. For five young Londoners, one day will bring panic, grief and conflict, and risks worth taking.

Lightning Source UK Ltd.
Milton Keynes UK
UKOW04f2048051214

242701UK00001B/10/P